W9-AKA-332

For all the underdogs

ME AND YOU
A DOUBLEDAY BOOK 978 0 385 61489 4

Published in Great Britain by Doubleday,
an imprint of Random House Children's Books
A Random House Group Company

This edition published 2010

3 5 7 9 10 8 6 4 2

RANDOM HOUSE CHILDREN'S BOOKS

61–63 Uxbridge Road, London W5 5SA

www.kidsatrandomhouse.co.uk

www.rbooks.co.uk

Addresses for companies within The Random House Group Limited can be found at:
www.randomhouse.co.uk/offices.htm

THE RANDOM HOUSE GROUP Limited Reg. No. 954009

A CIP catalogue record for this book is available from the British Library.

Printed and bound in Singapore

Anthony Browne

Me and You

Doubleday

This is our house.

There's Daddy Bear, Mummy Bear and me.

One morning Mummy made porridge for
breakfast, but it was too hot to eat.
"Let's all go out for a gentle stroll in the park
while it cools down," said Daddy. So we did.

3

The girl leaped out of bed, ran downstairs
and out of the door.

I wonder what happened to her?

"Oh no," Daddy said. "SOMEONE'S been in my bed!"
"Oh!" shrieked Mummy. "Someone's been in MY bed!"
"Someone's been in my bed," I said, "and they're STILL THERE!"

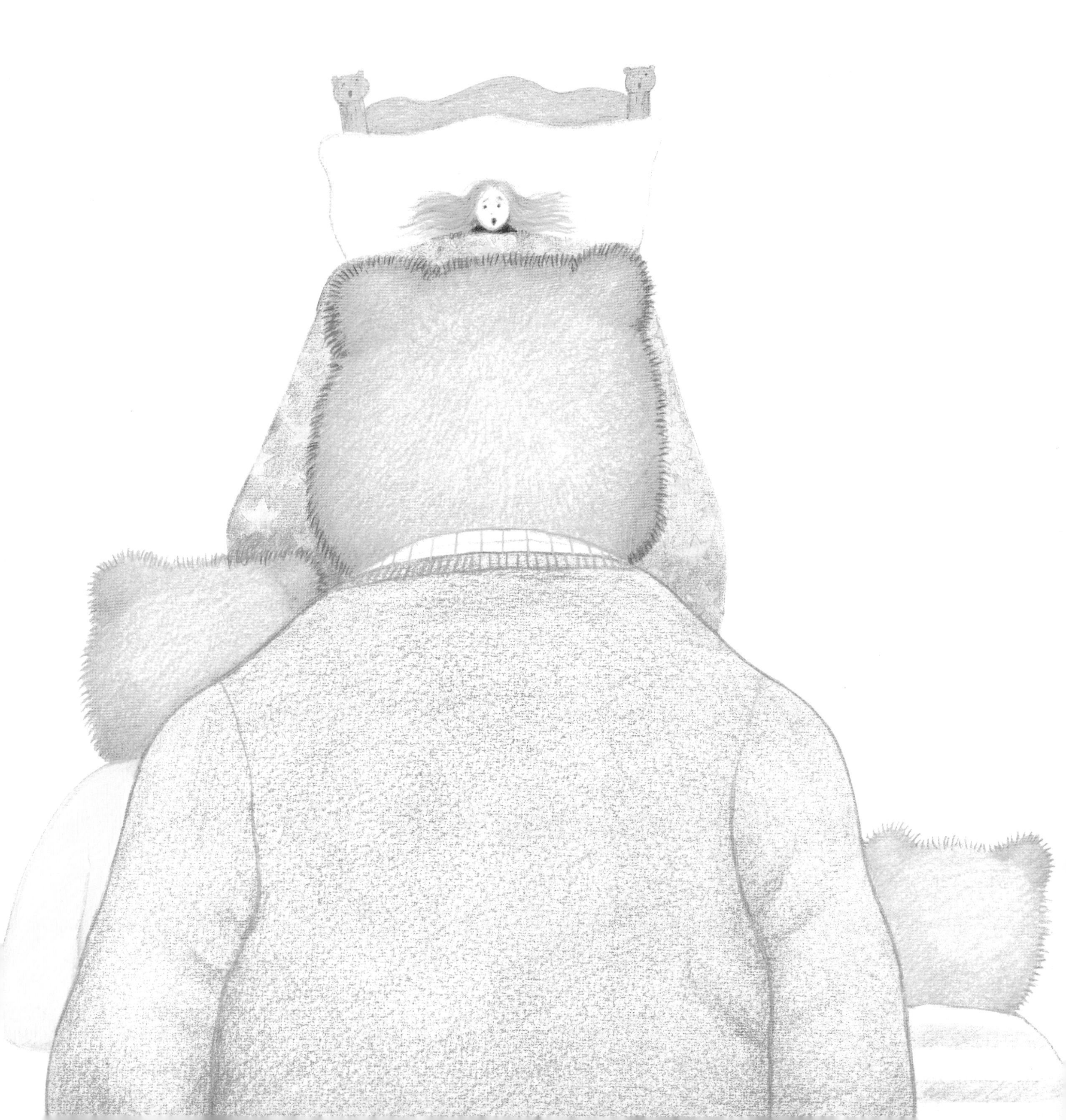

"Do be
careful,
dear,"
said
Daddy.

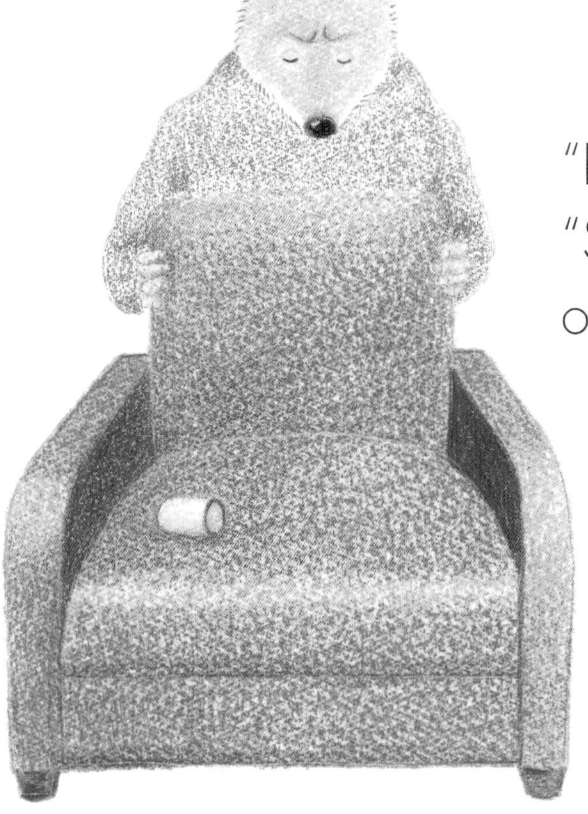

"Hang on a minute," said Daddy.
"Someone's been sitting
on my chair."

"Someone's been sitting
on MY chair!" said Mummy.

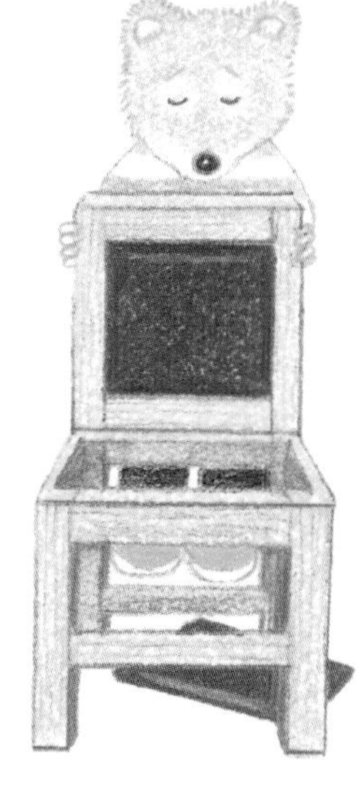

"Someone's been sitting on my chair
and they've BROKEN it!" I yelled.

"We'd better take a look upstairs,"
whispered Daddy. "After you, Mummy."

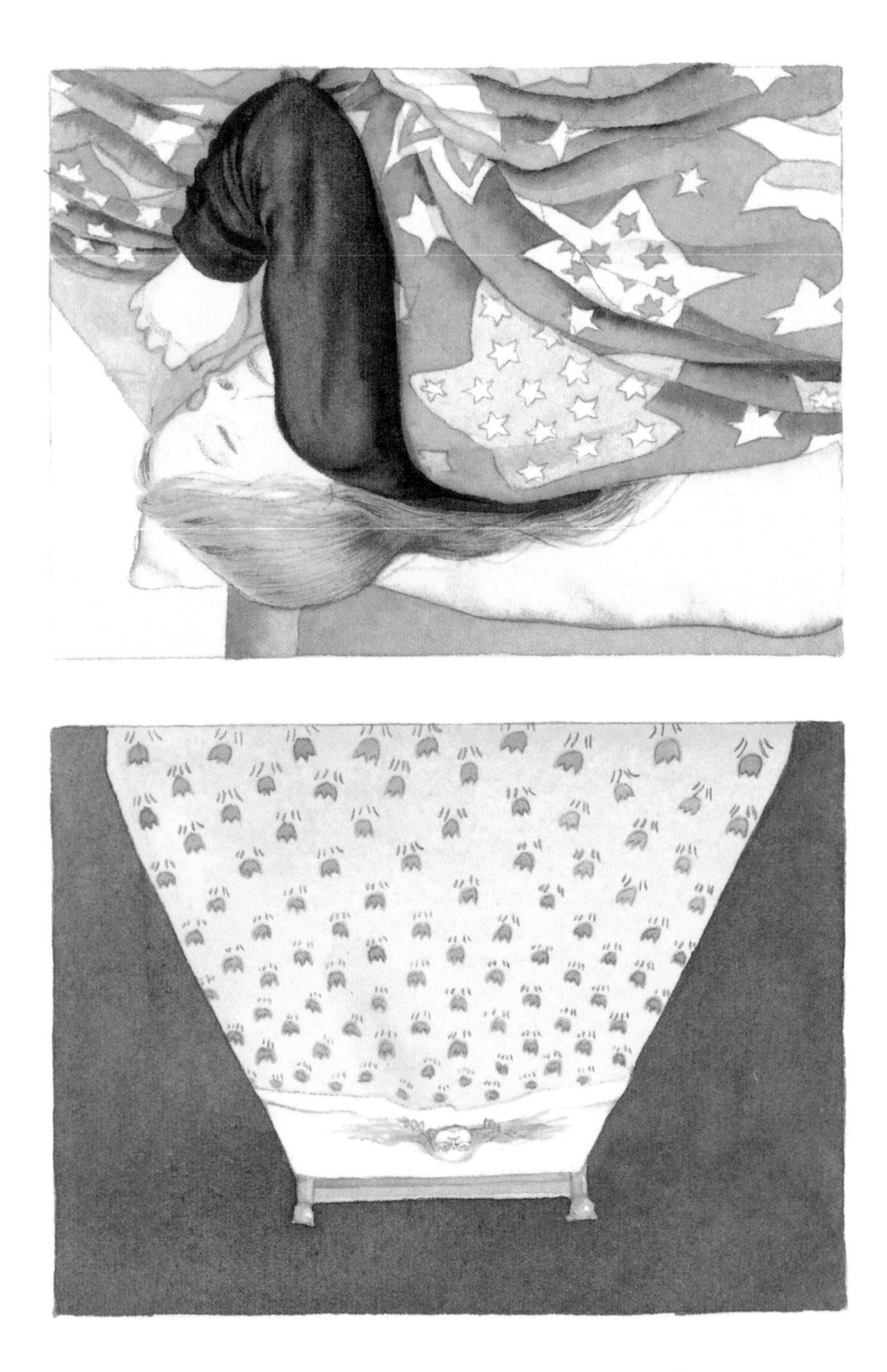
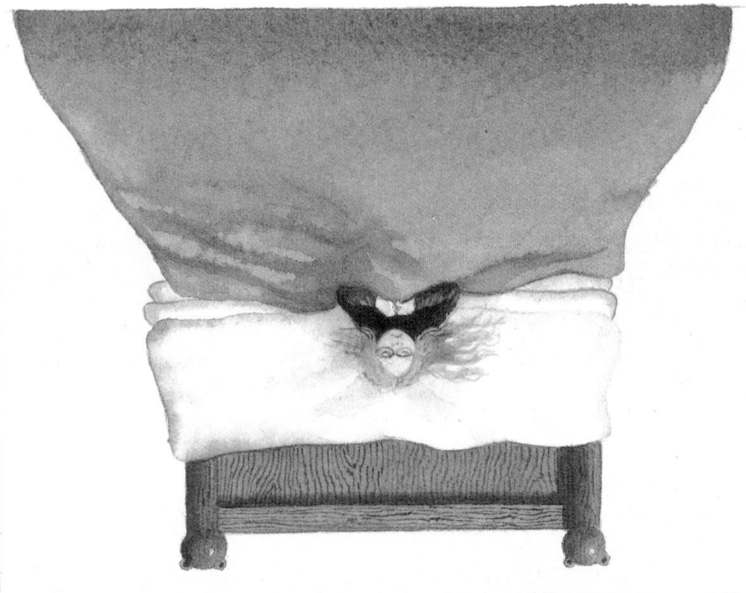

Daddy saw his spoon sticking out of his porridge.
"That's funny . . . " he said.
Mummy saw her spoon. "That's funny . . . " she said.
Then I saw that my bowl was empty. "That's not funny," I said. "Someone's eaten all my porridge."

When we got home, the front door was open.
Daddy said that Mummy must have left it open,
and Mummy said it must have been Daddy.
I didn't say anything.

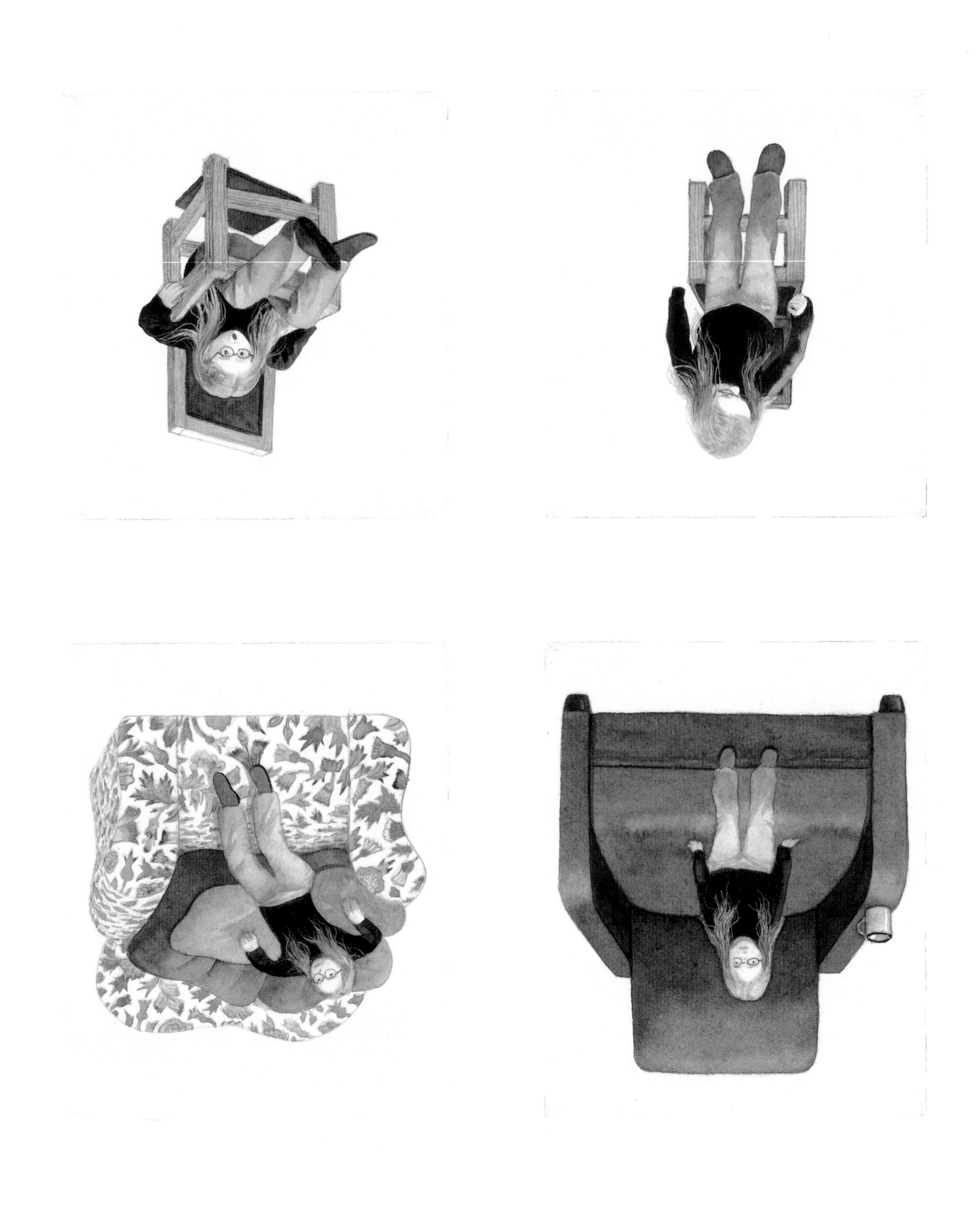

On the way back, Daddy talked about the car and
Mummy talked about the house. I just messed about.

Daddy talked about *his* work and Mummy talked about *her* work. I just messed about.